Classic Ghost Stories

Retold by Sheila Scott

Burlington Books

Classic Ghost Stories

Retold by Sheila Scott

Burlington Books
P. O. Box 54411
3721 Limassol
Cyprus
Burlington Books is an imprint of the Burlington Group.

The publisher gratefully acknowledges the following for providing photographs: © ASAP / Alamy: page 64, © Getty Images Israel / SSPL: page 14; © Shutterstock: cover; page 38, 41, 56, 65, 66, 67; © Wikipedia: page 41.

The publisher would like to thank the following people:

Castellano:	Alicia Ruiz Cuéllar
Català:	Maria Esteve Serraviñals
Euskara:	Edurne Azkue Urrestilla
Galego:	Ramón Nicolás Rodríguez

ISBN 978-9963-51-504-2

Burlington Reader No. NE4.15

10 9 8 7 6 5 4 3 2
25 24 23 22 21 20 19 18 17 16

CONTENTS

Introducción

En esta colección se ha reunido a tres autores clásicos para disfrutar de sus mejores relatos de fantasmas. En *The Signal-Man*, Charles Dickens (1812-1870) narra la historia de un guardavías al que constantemente se le aparece un fantasma en la entrada del túnel del tren que intenta avisarle de algo. Después de cada aparición ocurre un trágico suceso en la vía del tren. En *The Marble Finger*, E. Nesbit (1858-1924) relata la historia de un matrimonio joven que vive en una casa de campo de un tranquilo pueblo. No hacen caso de las advertencias de la asistenta acerca de una antigua maldición sobre unas estatuas de mármol que cobran vida en Halloween. Piensan que es una superstición y hacen caso omiso... ¡hasta que es demasiado tarde! En *The Body Snatcher*, Robert Louis Stevenson (1850-1894) cuenta cómo un estudiante de medicina se ve involucrado en una trama de tráfico de cadáveres que proporcionan a su facultad para su posterior estudio, ¿pero cómo los consiguen?

Introducció

En aquesta col·lecció s'apleguen tres autors clàssics per gaudir dels seus millors relats de fantasmes. A *The Signal-Man*, Charles Dickens (1812-1870) narra la història d'un guardaagulles a qui constantment se li apareix un fantasma a l'entrada del túnel del tren per intentar avisar-lo d'alguna cosa. Després de cada aparició té lloc un tràgic esdeveniment a la via del tren. A *The Marble Finger*, E. Nesbit (1858-1924) explica la història d'un matrimoni jove que viu a una casa de camp d'un poble tranquil. No fan cas de les advertències de l'assistenta sobre una antiga maledicció d'unes estàtues de marbre que cobren vida per Halloween. Creuen que es tracta d'una superstició i no hi paren atenció... fins que és massa tard! A *The Body Snatcher*, Robert Louis Stevenson (1850-1894) relata com un alumne de medicina es veu involucrat en una trama de tràfic de cadàvers que es proporcionen a la seva facultat per al seu estudi posterior, però com els aconsegueixen?

Sarrera

Bilduma honetan hiru idazle klasiko elkartu ditugu, beren mamuen istorio onenekin goza ahal izateko. *The Signal-Man* kontaketan, trenaren tunel-sarrera batean trenbide-zaindari bati etengabeki agertzen zaion eta zerbait jakinarazi nahi dion mamu baten istorioa kontatzen digu Charles Dickensek (1812-1870). Agerraldi bakoitzaren ondoren, trenbidean zorigaiztoa gertatzen da. *The Marble Finger* ipuinean, E. Nesbitek (1858-1924) herritxo lasai bateko landetxe batean bizi den senar-emazte gazte baten istorioa kontatzen digu. Neskameak Halloween gauean bizitza hartzen duten marmolezko estatua batzuei buruzko antzinako madarikazio batez ohartarazten dituenean, bikoteak ez dio jaramonik egingo. Superstizioa dela deritzo, eta ez du aintzat hartuko... beranduegi den arte! *The Body Snatcher* kontaketan, Robert Louis Stevensonek (1850-1894) kontatzen digu medikuntza-ikasle bat nola nahasi den bere fakultatera ikerketarako hilotzak hornitzen dituen gorpuen trafikoen konjurazio batean; baina nola lortzen ote dituzte gorpuak?

Limiar

Nesta colección xuntáronse tres autores clásicos para gozar dos seus mellores relatos de fantasmas. En *The Signal-Man*, Charles Dickens (1812-1870) narra a historia dun gardaagullas ao que recorrentemente se lle aparece un fantasma na entrada do túnel do tren que intenta avisalo de algo. Despois de cada aparición ocorre un tráxico suceso na vía do tren. En *The Marble Finger*, E. Nesbit (1858-1924) relata a historia dun matrimonio novo que vive nunha casa de campo dunha vila tranquila. Non fan caso das advertencias da asistenta arredor dunha antiga maldición sobre unhas estatuas de mármore que cobran vida en Halloween. Pensan que é unha superstición e fan caso omiso... até que é tarde de máis! En *The Body Snatcher*, Robert Louis Stevenson (1850-1894) conta como un estudante de medicina vai verse involucrado nunha trama de tráfico de cadáveres que proporcionan á súa facultade para o seu posterior estudo mais, como os conseguen?

The Signal-Man

by Charles Dickens

PRE-READING ACTIVITIES

1 Complete the text with the words below.

lonely paths warn reached deep prevented danger depressing

In the past, a signal-man's job was to 1. .... train drivers if there was any 2. .... on the railway lines. It was important work that 3. .... accidents, but it was solitary work for the signal-men. Some of them felt very 4. .... with no one nearby. Some signal boxes were so remote that signal-men had to walk kilometres along small 5. .... to get to work. Sometimes, a signal-man's box was situated in a 6. .... valley and light from the sun never 7. .... it. Then, the signal-man worked all day in a gloomy and 8. .... atmosphere.

2 How do you think a signal-man's mind could be affected by being alone for a long time?

....

....

....

3 How do you think a signal-man would feel about an unexpected visitor?

....

....

....

CHAPTER 1

A Long-Planned Visit

When I was a busy doctor, I didn't have much time to travel around the country. However, on the rare occasions when I travelled, I went by train. I've always liked trains and railways. I'm impressed by the clever engineering that cuts tunnels for railway lines out of hillsides. Until the events of this story, I was also fascinated by the signal system and wanted to know more about the work of the signal-men, and how they controlled it.

"One day, I'll go and talk to some of those signal-men about their work," I promised myself. I had no idea at the time that this would lead to a **nightmare** I would live with for the rest of my life.

About six months before I retired, the newspapers were full of reports of a terrible train accident in a railway tunnel in the south of England. Everybody was talking about it. Who was responsible? How did it happen? I decided that it was time for my long-planned visit to the signal-men. I was strongly **compelled** to visit the site of the accident in the south of England.

"That's where I'll start," I said to myself, and started to search for places to stay in that area. I found a small **inn** not far from the site of the accident and made a reservation there.

I arrived at the inn in the afternoon, and left almost at once for the railway. It was a beautiful summer afternoon, and everything looked bright under a cloudless blue sky. When I reached the railway **cutting** and looked down, I was shocked by the contrast.

The cutting was deep with stony sides. No sunlight reached the bottom. A **signal box** stood near the entrance to a dark, **gloomy** tunnel. "What a depressing place to work," I thought to myself. "It's so dark and cold. I feel sorry for the signal-man."

As I stood there, the earth began to vibrate and a train suddenly emerged from the tunnel and rushed past. When the sound of the engine **faded** in the distance, I called down to the signal-man, "Hello down there!"

The man was surprised. He stared up at me, but said nothing. "He doesn't seem pleased to see me," I thought. "I'm surprised he isn't happy to have a visitor in this lonely place." I smiled down at him and shouted again, "Is there a path I can use to come down and speak to you?"

The signal-man pointed with his flag to a place some distance from where I stood. I saw there was a **rough** path cut into the hillside, and this led down to the railway line. Carefully, I climbed down the **steep** path till I reached the bottom. In that damp-smelling place, I suddenly felt chilled by the cold wind, or perhaps I was chilled by the look on the signal-man's face. I can still see it in my mind. He looked terrified.

"Don't fear me," I said. "I assure you, I'm a simple, honest man."

"You look familiar," he said, suspiciously. "Have you been here before?"

"My dear fellow," I said, "I've never been here in my life. In fact, this is the first time I've ever visited this part of the country."

I called down to the signal-man, "Hello down there!"

My reply seemed to calm him. He led me into a small room inside the signal box. There was a welcoming fire there. On the desk, there was a notebook, a telegraphic instrument to communicate with other signal-men and a little bell. He said, "The bell rings when there is a message for me, or to warn of some trouble on the line." I asked the signal-man questions about his work, and he answered **willingly**. He took his job very seriously. "He's a responsible man," I thought. "But he seems too well-educated for this job. Why isn't he working in a more pleasant place or in a more interesting job?"

I decided to ask him about it.

"I was foolish when I was young," he explained. "I wasn't serious about studying, and I **wasted** my time and opportunities. I can't find a better job without an education, but this job is not so bad. I must **earn a living** and I've become accustomed to it."

"Isn't it very lonely down here?" I asked.

"Yes, it *is* lonely," he replied. "But it's my nature to be solitary. Now I've got time to study. I've taught myself French and some maths."

I liked the fellow, and his responsible attitude impressed me greatly. While we were talking, the bell rang several times. This showed that other signal-men were sending messages. I watched while he read the messages on his machine, and then sent his replies.

CHAPTER 2

Strange Behaviour

Our conversation was very pleasant, but my new friend behaved very strangely on two occasions. He stopped talking suddenly as if he heard the bell ring – but the bell *did not* ring. There was no sound in the signal box or outside, besides the wind. Did he hear something that I didn't? He got up, opened the door and looked towards the entrance to the tunnel. When he returned to his chair, his face was white. "He's had a shock," I thought. "He looks really frightened. What did he see out there?"

When it happened for a second time, I asked gently, "Is anything wrong?"

He stopped talking suddenly as if he heard the bell ring – but the bell did not *ring.*

"I'm **distressed**, sir, deeply distressed," he replied. Then, he shook his head and said, "But I can't talk about it."

I didn't try to persuade him to speak. In my experience as a doctor, when a person is in distress, it's better to be patient and wait until they're ready to talk. After a few minutes, he said, "If you come again tomorrow evening, I'll try to explain." I promised to come after supper, and got up to leave.

I was surprised when he said, "I'll shine my light on the path until you reach the top, but please don't shout when you get there."

Then he asked me a strange question, "What made you shout '*Hello down there!*' when you arrived here?"

"I wanted to attract your attention," I replied.

"I understand that," said the signal-man. "But why did you choose those exact words? Did you have a feeling that they entered your head in a supernatural way?"

"No, I didn't," I said, surprised. "I've no idea why I chose those words." Surely, the man didn't believe in supernatural influences! He seemed too intelligent for that.

I didn't sleep well that night. Over and over again, images of the man's frightened face ran through my head. I thought again about his strange behaviour.

"What was he afraid of?" I wondered. "Why did he behave as if he heard the bell when it didn't ring? Why did he tell me not to shout from the top of the path?"

I understood that the man was very distressed, and as a doctor I know that distress can sometimes lead to irrational behaviour. I couldn't think of a rational explanation for his actions, so I hoped he would explain everything on my next visit to him.

The next evening, we sat by the fire and the signal-man told me what was troubling him. But he didn't speak like the practical, intelligent man I thought he was. Instead, he spoke of ghosts. "I see figures around the entrance to the train tunnel," he explained. "They aren't human. They must be ghosts because when I approach them, they suddenly disappear. Each time, I search the tunnel but they aren't there, and there's nowhere else for them to go." Then he added, "Terrible events always follow their appearance."

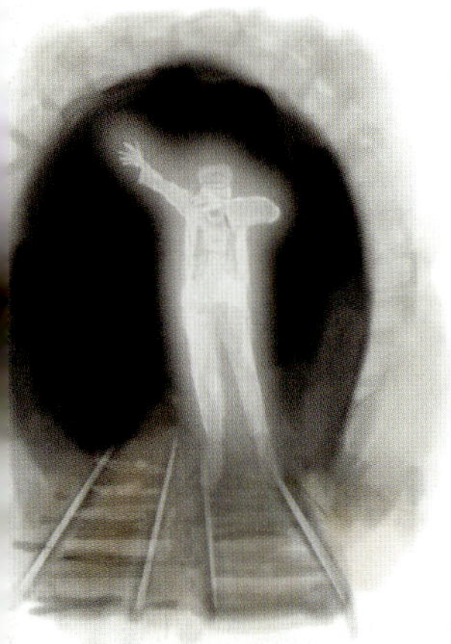

A man stood with his left arm over his face.

"On the first occasion, a man stood with his left arm over his face. He **waved** his right arm violently in a gesture of 'Clear the way, clear the way.' He shouted, 'Hello down there,' and added a warning, '**Look out!** Look out!' Then, he disappeared. A few hours later, there was a terrible accident in the tunnel."

"How strange," I thought. "When I came here yesterday, I also shouted, 'Hello down there!' So, that's why the signal-man looked terrified. He thought I was another ghost!"

"Surely, it was coincidence that I used the ghost's words?" I thought, though I've never believed in coincidence. Then, I thought again about the terrible train accident in that area. "Why did I feel compelled to come here, to this place?" I wondered. They were uncomfortable thoughts, but I could not ignore them.

The signal-man continued his story. "The ghost was trying to warn me," he said, quietly, "but what could I do? I didn't know what the warning meant, or what to do about it.

"One morning, a few months later, the ghost appeared again. This time, it had its hands over its face in a gesture of **mourning**. The ghost also disappeared in a mysterious way, and later that day, a young woman on a train died very suddenly as the train passed through the tunnel. Her body was brought to the signal box.

"The ghost warned me there would be a tragedy," he said. "But why? I couldn't prevent the woman's death."

I wondered if these warnings were actually predictions – a bit like '**second sight**', where people 'see' events before they happen. If so, there was nothing the signal-man, or anyone else, could do to prevent the disasters.

I decided to say nothing. I was **relieved** that the second ghost didn't use those **fateful** words, "Hello down there!" Here at least, there was no connection to myself.

Still, I was worried. "If the warnings actually happened, it would be very frightening," I thought, "and if he only imagined them, it is difficult to understand how they were both followed so closely by terrible events."

Something weird was happening and I didn't like it. I didn't like it at all.

The ghost had its hands over its face in a gesture of mourning.

1 Replace the bolded words with the synonyms below.

wonder rushed pleased chilled weird approached

1. The stories he told me were **strange**.

   ....

2. As I **came near to** the man, I saw he wasn't smiling.

   ....

3. John was **happy** that they had a room for him at the inn.

   ....

4. When he saw the body, he suddenly felt **cold**.

   ....

5. The train **travelled very quickly** out of the tunnel.

   ....

6. I often **ask myself** if the man is still driving trains.

   ....

2 Circle the most logical words to complete the sentences.

1. Doctors who treat mental health problems study **human engineering** / **human behaviour** / **hillsides**.
2. He looked unhappy, and I asked what was **pointing** / **leading** / **troubling** him.
3. The signal-man waved his **flag** / **earth** / **death** after he saw the broken railway line.
4. He **shone** / **stared up** / **behaved** the light on the picture.
5. His **uncomfortable** / **clever** / **foolish** idea worked very well.

Did you know?

Robert Stephenson's engine *Invicta* provided the power for the first regular passenger service in the world. It started in 1830 and travelled from Canterbury to Whitstable in Kent, England – a distance of six miles (9.6 kilometres).

3 The following statements about the story are false. Underline the incorrect part of the sentences and then correct them.

1. The doctor's decision about which signal box to visit was based on advice from a friend.

   ....

2. The doctor thought the signal box was a pleasant place to work.

   ....

3. The signal-man took the job because he was a responsible person.

   ....

4. The signal-man said he could never explain his problem.

   ....

5. The ghosts gave warnings, but nothing terrible happened.

   ....

4 The setting is the time and place that a story takes place. Where does this story take place? What do you think is the time period of the story?

....

....

....

5 Answer the questions. Write the answers in your notebook.

1. Why hadn't the doctor visited a signal box before?
2. What surprised the doctor when he called down to the signal-man?
3. Why did the signal-man ask the doctor about supernatural influences?
4. Why was the signal-man so sure that the figures he saw were ghosts?

CHAPTER 3

A Difficult Decision

I have had a long experience with human nature, and I usually know when a person is lying. I was sure the signal-man was telling the truth, or at least what he believed was the truth. Sometimes, a distressed person confuses imagination with reality, but this didn't fit with my impression of the man.

"There must be another explanation," I thought.

The signal-man told me his news. "The ghost returned a few days before your visit," he told me. "It appears every day now." Sometimes at the top of the path, sometimes near the entrance to the tunnel. It shouts, 'Hello down there!' and warns me, 'Look out! Look out!'"

"*Hello down there!* – those words again," I thought, and this time I felt an uncontrollable fear.

"It calls and waves its arms, just as before, and sometimes my bell rings," said the signal-man. "I know it's warning me of future danger but nothing has happened."

Terrible thoughts entered my mind. "What's going to happen? Will someone else die?" I thought about the bells. To me they were silent, but the signal-man heard them ring and left the signal box immediately on each occasion. That was when he saw the ghost and came back looking so distressed.

"Enough!" I said to myself, firmly. "Supernatural events are nonsense." But were they nonsense? I was no longer sure.

The signal-man looked at me. "What should I do?" he asked. "It's my **duty** to warn my superiors of danger, but if I tell them this, they'll think my mind is **unbalanced**, and I'll lose my job."

I wanted to help the poor fellow. I didn't think he was unbalanced, but maybe the long hours alone in this cold, depressing place were affecting him. I tried to calm him.

"Is it possible that the figures were optical illusions, and the voices the sound of the wind in the tunnel?" I asked quietly, trying to convince myself, as well as my new friend. But I was unsuccessful in both cases.

I really hoped he was imagining everything, but something, deep inside me, told me he was not.

I didn't like to leave the man in such a state, so I offered to stay in the signal box with him until morning. He didn't accept my offer. I'll never forgive myself for agreeing to leave. Again, he shone his light up the path to help me see my way in the darkness, and I shouted goodbye.

He shone his light up the path to help me see my way in the darkness.

I walked back to the inn, preoccupied with the signal-man's stories, and tried to push thoughts of ghosts and supernatural figures out of my mind. I had a practical decision to make. The safety of trains and the lives of passengers depended on this signal-man. If there was any possibility that his mind was affected by his troubles, his superiors should know about it. I didn't think the signal-man was unbalanced, but his distress could affect his work, and put people's lives in danger.

"Perhaps it's my duty to tell them," I thought. "But how can I **betray** the man's confidence? It's not ethical. On the other hand, is it safe for him to be responsible for a railway line and the passengers that travel on it?"

I decided not to talk to the signal-man's superiors yet. Instead, I would take him to a medical colleague of mine, an expert in mental health problems. "After that, I'll decide what to do," I told myself, firmly.

I felt better after making that decision and was finally able to sleep for a few hours.

CHAPTER 4

A Strange, Quiet Fellow

The next day, I talked to the innkeeper about the accident in that area. "It was terrible," he said. "Eight people died and about 20 were hurt. They put them beside the signal box. It seems someone forgot to report a break on one of the rails. That's what caused the accident."

The conversation didn't help my **mood** that day. In the evening, the innkeeper's wife served me a nice supper, but I ate the food without tasting a thing.

After supper, I walked quickly to the railway and looked down. I was almost **overcome** with horror. Standing at the entrance to the tunnel there was a figure with its left arm over its eyes, waving its right arm dramatically, exactly as the signal-man described.

"Dear Lord," I thought in terror, "it's the ghost!"

Almost at once, I realised it wasn't a supernatural figure at all, but a real man. There was a small group of other men standing near him. He was gesturing and repeating the gesture to demonstrate something to them.

Near them on the ground, there was a small platform made of wood. It was covered with a heavy cloth. I was filled with a terrible fear. Something was very wrong. Where was the signal-man? I climbed down the path as fast as I could.

Something was very wrong.

"What's wrong?" I asked the men when I arrived at the tunnel. "I'm a doctor. Can I help?"

"A signal-man was killed this morning," one of them replied.

I was shocked, but not greatly surprised. "We knew a disaster was going to happen," I thought. "But how did we know?" The answer was disturbing. We knew because the ghost gave my friend the warning. But wasn't the ghost nonsense?

"I shouted and shouted as loud as I could, but he didn't seem to hear," the driver replied.

"Did the dead man work in the signal box?" I asked.

"Yes, sir," he said. "That's correct. He was a strange, quiet fellow."

"How did it happen?" I asked.

"It's a terrible thing. I don't understand it," the train driver said. "He was always so careful, but he was standing in the middle of the railway line in front of my train, and he didn't move as we came closer. I only saw him as we came out of the tunnel and it was too late to slow down. There was nothing I could do."

"But did he not hear anything?" I asked.

"I shouted and shouted as loud as I could, but he didn't seem to hear," the driver replied. "I waved my right arm until the last moment. When I saw it was no use, I covered my eyes with my left arm, like this, not to see." He put his left arm across his eyes.

I was afraid to ask, but I wanted to be sure. I knew what the answer would be. My own words echoed in my head.

"What did you say when you shouted?" I asked, fearfully.

"I shouted, 'Hello down there! Look out! Look out!'" the driver replied.

There was nothing more for me to say.

CHAPTERS 3-4 ACTIVITIES

1 The bolded words are in the wrong sentences. Write each word after the correct sentence.

1. I think it is **unsuccessful** to believe in supernatural beings.

   ....

2. I don't know what was in the box but it was **darkness**.

   ....

3. I tried to help the man but I was **heavy**.

   ....

4. The three men put the body down and **didn't fit** it.

   ....

5. When they work in **confidence**, signal-men use torches.

   ....

6. His face was white and I **covered** he was very distressed.

   ....

7. He was a good doctor and I had great **nonsense** in him.

   ....

8. His behaviour **realised** with my opinion of him.

   ....

2 Complete the sentences with the words below.

lying | *wood* | *forgive* | *slow down* | *ground* | *cloths*

1. I will never .... myself for not helping the man.
2. We walked across the wet .... to the old house.
3. I knew he was .... because he refused to look at me.
4. Trains have to .... when they get near a station.
5. Nobody lived in the house and there were big .... over all the furniture.
6. In the mountains, the houses were all made of ....

3 Number the sentences in the correct order according to the story.

.... a. The signal-man asked his visitor for advice.

.... b. For a moment, the doctor thought he was seeing a ghost.

.... c. A train driver described a terrible experience.

.... d. The innkeeper told the doctor about the earlier train accident.

.... e. The doctor began to doubt his own opinions.

.... f. The signal-man refused an offer of help.

.... g. The doctor fell asleep after making his decision.

4 A conflict is a struggle between two opposing forces, for example between a person's feelings and what he / she knows is the correct thing to do. Answer the questions.

1. After hearing the signal-man's story, what conflict did the doctor have?

   ....

2. How did the doctor resolve his conflict?

   ....

5 Answer the questions. Write the answers in your notebook.

1. Why was the doctor not surprised to hear that the signal-man had died?
2. According to the train driver, what was unusual about the signal-man's behaviour?
3. Why did the doctor ask the train driver which words he had shouted?

Did you know?

The worst train accident in the United Kingdom happened in 1915 near Gretna Green, Scotland. More than 200 people were killed. An investigation found that it was caused by the signal-men not following the correct procedure.

The Marble Finger

based on the novel ***Man-made in Marble***
by E. Nesbit

PRE-READING ACTIVITIES

1 Complete the text with the words and phrases below.

turned into | *knight* | *furniture* | *footsteps* | *aware of* | *for a living* | *locking*

I sell second-hand [1] .... as well as ornaments and old paintings, [2] .... My work was always fun, but last week, it [3] .... something frightening, when things in the shop started to move! I first became [4] .... it when I was [5] .... the front door of the shop one night and heard [6] .... inside. I thought it was my imagination, but next morning, I found the little statue of a [7] .... standing near the front door, instead of on the shelf where I had put it.

2 Do you agree with the following statements? Explain your answers. Write your explanations in your notebook.

1. Legends develop through time to explain events that do not have a logical explanation.
2. Legends are passed down orally, and therefore the stories often become exaggerated.
3. After evil men die, their spirits continue to be dangerous.
4. It is possible to die of fright.
5. It is acceptable to take money from a dishonest source if the money is going to a good cause.

PROLOGUE

This is the story of my life's tragedy. Although every word of it is true, I don't think readers will believe it. Nowadays, people want rational explanations for everything that happens. If they hear a story that mentions the occult, or describes supposedly unnatural events, they think the speaker was drunk or mentally unbalanced at the time the events took place.

Three people took part in this story. The other one who is still alive can testify to the truth of these events. Readers must decide for themselves what to believe.

CHAPTER 1

A New Home in the Country

At the time these events took place, I painted pictures for a living and my beloved wife, Laura, wrote poems. It was clear to us before we married that we couldn't make enough money to live in the city.

"Never mind," said Laura. "We can be just as happy in the country."

I looked at her lovingly and wondered, How did I find such a wonderful girl? She's going to be a perfect wife.

A few weeks before the wedding, we began our search for a cottage in the country. We contacted **estate agents** in different places and went to look at several places. Our demands were simple enough – a cottage that was picturesque and sanitary. The agents seemed to have difficulty understanding these demands. They showed us cottages which looked lovely on the outside, but were extremely primitive inside. The modern cottages we saw frequently looked like biscuit boxes.

After our wedding, we were on honeymoon, and we heard about a cottage in Brenzett. Since it was not too far from the seaside village where we were staying, we went to see it, fully expecting to be disappointed once again.

To our amazement, the cottage was delightful! Two rooms remained of the large house that had once stood there. The rest of the long, low building had been added later and was modern and comfortable inside. The outside stone work was covered with green plants and pink roses. It was charming.

We spent the last few days of our honeymoon searching in the nearby village shops for good second-hand furniture. It was mid-summer when we moved into our new home, and we were very happy. I never got tired of painting the view from the window and Laura wrote her poems, mostly about love.

Neither of us had much domestic talent, but fortunately, we found an old local woman, Mrs Dorman, to do the **housekeeping**. Her cooking skills were limited, but she compensated for this with her wonderful local legends. Some were so fascinating that Laura turned them into magazine stories, which brought us a welcome extra salary.

I never got tired of painting the view from the window.

Many of Mrs Dorman's stories were about 'things that walked at night' and 'strange sights'. She clearly believed every word of them. Laura and I listened with pleasure and were careful not to show any scepticism. Over a smoke and a drink, I discussed the stories with our neighbour, the local doctor. We exchanged a few laughs and agreed that Mrs Dorman was a great storyteller.

For several months, Laura and I enjoyed perfect married happiness and never fought. I painted, Laura wrote and Mrs Dorman did the housekeeping.

But one day, I returned from a short walk to find Laura in tears.

"My darling," I said, holding out my arms to her. "What's wrong? What happened?"

"It's Mrs Dorman," she replied through her tears. "She's leaving to help her sick niece. I'll have to do the cooking and housekeeping myself, and you know how useless I am!"

I hated to see my darling Laura unhappy.

"Don't cry, darling," I begged her. "I'll clean and help you with the cooking. When is Mrs Dorman leaving?"

"On Thursday," she replied. It was some time before I could calm her, and I promised to speak to Mrs Dorman the next day.

CHAPTER 2

Mrs Dorman's Warning

I took Laura's hand and said, "Come, it's a beautiful evening. Let's go for a walk and forget about Mrs Dorman for a while."

Our walk took us along a familiar and much loved route. We followed a path through a little forest and across a field to the **churchyard**. The path beside the churchyard wall was called 'the **coffin**-walk' because it led from the church to the churchyard. It was shaded by majestic tall trees.

We often went into the church, which was old and very beautiful. It was only used on Sundays, but the heavy doors were never locked. Inside, we admired the high arched roof, the heavy dark seats and the magnificent glass windows.

On either side of the altar, on **marble** pedestals, were two life-size figures of knights in armour, **carved** from grey marble. The two men had cruel faces, but their hands were held up in lasting prayer. Perhaps they were praying for forgiveness for all their **evil deeds**.

On either side of the altar, on marble pedestals, were two life-size figures of knights in armour.

Villagers told us they had been cruel men much hated by the local people. They had lived in a big house where our cottage now stood. Vengeance for their wicked deeds came when lightning **struck** the house and destroyed most of it. Apparently, the knights' evil deeds were deliberately ignored when their **heirs** bought them their important places in the church, using the gold of their ancestors' crimes!

Next day, I kept my promise to Laura, and spoke to our housekeeper.

"Mrs Dorman," I said. "I'm very sorry to hear that your niece is ill, but must you leave so soon? Perhaps you could wait a while."

I could see the old woman was uncomfortable when she replied, "No sir – I'm sorry. I have to go before Thursday."

"Is your salary not high enough?" I asked gently, thinking perhaps this was the real reason she was leaving.

This time, she replied quickly, "Oh no, sir. I'm paid quite enough." Then she added, "I may be able to come back next week."

It was clear the woman was hiding something, and I was determined to discover the real reason. "Mrs Dorman, why must you go this week?" I asked. "Please tell me the truth."

It took a bit more persuasion, but eventually she said, "Well sir, bad deeds were done in this house, and I want to be far away from it on Halloween, **All Saints' Eve**."

I was confused by her reply, and I wanted to hear more.

"Mrs Dorman, why must you go this week?" I asked. "Please tell me the truth."

She **hesitated**, and then looked at me. "Have you seen those stone figures of the knights in the church?" she asked. "On All Saints' Eve, at exactly 11 o'clock, they get down from their pedestals, walk out of the church, along the coffin-walk and come here to this house where they once lived."

She trembled as she continued, "If they see or meet anyone ..."

She didn't complete the sentence, and I was left to imagine what horrible things happened to these unfortunate souls. Since I didn't believe her tale, I was not particularly worried, but I hid my scepticism.

"Has anyone ever seen these figures here?" I asked.

"That's not for me to say, sir, but I know what I know," she said.

"What about the lady who lived here last year? Didn't she see the figures?" I wanted to know.

"The lady was only here in the summer," she replied.

Mrs Dorman got up to leave, and then she turned to give one last warning. I remember her words as if they were burnt on my brain. There is not a day since then that I don't think of them and feel a powerful sense of responsibility because I didn't listen to her warnings.

"Whatever you do, sir," she said, "be very careful on Friday night. It's Halloween. Lock all the doors early and mark a cross over the door and on the windows."

I didn't tell Laura what Mrs Dorman had said. She was nervous by nature and I didn't want to frighten her. Although I didn't take the warning seriously, a cold shiver ran down my spine.

Mrs Dorman left, and much to my surprise, for the next few days Laura cooked delicious meals. I prepared vegetables for her and cleaned the house. The experience of housekeeping was new for us, and we did it together, laughing when things went wrong. We enjoyed ourselves, happy to remember it was only for a short time.

"Whatever you do, sir," she said, "be very careful on Friday night. It's Halloween."

CHAPTERS 1-2 ACTIVITIES

1 Match the words in A to the correct definitions in B.

A	B
1. honeymoon	.... a. the part of the body you use to think
2. amazement	.... b. the cover on a building
3. lightning	.... c. a family member who lived before you were born
4. brain	.... d. an area near the ocean
5. seaside	.... e. a ceremony when people get married
6. wedding	.... f. a feeling of surprise
7. ancestor	.... g. a holiday after getting married
8. roof	.... h. a bright flash in the sky during a storm

2 Circle the correct continuation for each sentence. Pay attention to the words in bold.

1. She was **getting tired**.
   a. She had worked for hours.
   b. She had slept all night.
2. David was **charming**.
   a. It was easy to dislike him.
   b. Everybody liked him.
3. It was a **pleasure** talking to him.
   a. He was very interesting.
   b. I was bored listening to him.
4. It was **useless** trying to open the door.
   a. The key was broken.
   b. It was very easy.
5. We were **disappointed** with the show.
   a. We enjoyed it so much.
   b. We left before the end.

3 Write T (true) or F (false) next to each sentence. Then correct the false sentences.

.... 1. The cottage was not very far from the sea.

.... 2. It wasn't necessary to buy furniture for the cottage.

.... 3. Mrs Dorman was an excellent cook.

.... 4. Laura did not know the real reason why Mrs Dorman was leaving.

.... 5. The couple were unhappy while doing the cooking and cleaning.

.... 6. The 'coffin-walk' got its name from a local legend.

.... 7. Although it was only used on Sundays, the church was never locked.

.... 8. Evil men had burnt down the old house where the cottage now stood.

....

....

....

....

....

4 What happened as a result of the following? Write the answers in your notebook.

1. The young couple didn't have much money.
2. Laura was impressed by legends the housekeeper related.
3. Mrs Dorman left her housekeeping job.
4. The lady who lived there before, only stayed at the cottage in the summer.
5. The evil men's heirs bought places in the church for them.

Did you know?

The word 'honeymoon' is made up from the word 'honey,' which was used to make a sweet drink thousands of years ago, and the word 'moon', which is a lunar month. In medieval Europe, neighbours provided the newly-married couple with a month's supply of the drink which was supposed to have aphrodisiac powers.

CHAPTER 3

Halloween

On Friday evening, the night of Halloween, everything changed. Laura seemed tired and her bright happy smile had disappeared.

"Are you sad, my dearest?" I asked her.

"Not exactly sad," she said, slowly. "But I've got a bad feeling."

Then she added, "Have you ever had a premonition that something bad is going to happen?"

"No," I said immediately, without adding that I thought premonitions were nonsense, as Laura obviously believed in them.

"I remember what happened with my grandfather," she said, slowly. "He was far away in Scotland, and one day, I had a strong feeling something was wrong. We heard later that was the day he fell off his horse and died."

I didn't reply, but noticed that Laura was trembling.

"I've shivered three or four times this evening, and it isn't cold," she continued. But a little while later, she smiled, took my hand and kissed my cheek.

"Come on," she said. "Let's light the candles. I'll play the piano and we can sing duets."

I knew she was making an effort not to distress me, and after a while, I said, "Go to bed, dearest. I'll smoke my pipe for a bit. I won't be long."

I sat outside, smoking my pipe and thinking about my life.

"How lucky I am to have such a wonderful wife," I thought, and I was filled with a deep feeling of gratitude and satisfaction.

Around me, all was quiet. There were dark clouds in the sky, but no wind. In the distance, beyond the forests and the field, I saw the tall **spire** of the church. I'm not a religious man, but suddenly, I was filled with a powerful impulse.

"I must go to the church and give thanks to God for all his blessings," I thought.

I looked through the window, and saw that Laura had fallen asleep while reading, in the armchair beside the fire.

"She'll sleep well now," I thought to myself. "She's very tired."

In the distance, beyond the forests and the field, I saw the tall spire of the church.

It wouldn't take long to walk to the church if I walked fast. The church bell struck 11:00 as I left the house. It was only later that I connected the hour with Mrs Dorman's story. I was walking along the path beside the forest when I heard an unfamiliar sound. I stopped to listen and the sound stopped too. I started to walk again, and was aware of other footsteps on the path, like an echo of my own. I turned into the forest, and the footsteps continued.

"Maybe it's a **poacher**," I thought. They had caught a poacher in the forest just a few weeks before, but it seemed unlikely a poacher would step loudly enough to be heard. They knew how to move silently. I felt uncomfortable and a little nervous. I hurried through the forests and across the field. As I came near to the church, I saw the doors were wide open.

"No one comes here but Laura and I, except on a Sunday," I said to myself. "Did we forget to close the door on our last visit?"

I entered the church and walked down the **aisle** towards the altar. The moon came out and shone through the windows. My heart beat fast and I nearly **choked**. The marble pedestals on either side of the altar were empty! The two life-size marble knights were gone!

"Am I **insane**?" I asked myself. "Am I imagining this?"

I wondered if someone was **playing a trick**. "Those statues were heavy," I thought. "It would take several people to lift them. But why would anyone do such a thing?"

The two life-size marble knights were gone!

I moved closer to be sure. There was no doubt – the figures were gone. Mrs Dorman's words came back to me, "On All Saints' Eve, at exactly 11 o'clock, they get down from their pedestals, walk out of the church, along the coffin-walk and come here, to the house where they once lived."

An indescribable horror filled me and I ran out of the church and down the coffin-walk as fast as I could. I had to get home to Laura!

When I reached the field, I saw a dark figure and I shouted loudly, "Move! Get out of the way!" The figure didn't move, and I pushed it, but my arms were **grasped** and I heard the voice of my neighbour, the doctor.

"Hey," he said. "What's wrong? Why are you hurrying?"

"Let me go!" I shouted. "I must go! The marble knights have gone from the church! They've gone, I tell you!"

The doctor laughed. "Do you really believe those old wives' tales – or did you drink too much?" he asked.

"No, no, it's true, I tell you," I insisted. "The pedestals are empty. Let me go. I must go home to my wife."

"Come with me, my friend," he said. "Let's go to the church and you can show me what you saw there."

His strong hand and quiet voice calmed me a bit and I agreed to do what he suggested.

CHAPTER 4

Waiting by the Window

I let the doctor lead me into the church and up the aisle towards the altar. I shut my eyes. I knew the figures were gone and was afraid to see those empty pedestals again. I didn't know what it meant; only that it was something horrible.

Then, I heard his voice, "Here you are! See for yourself!"

I opened my eyes and there they were – the two stone figures on their pedestals. Breathing heavily, I caught the doctor's hand and said, "Thank you – thank you! What a **relief**! Maybe it was an optical illusion, or I'm just overworked, but I was quite convinced they were gone."

I think the doctor was worried about me although he didn't say so. "Come on, my friend," he said. "I'll walk home with you." Perhaps he thought I was unbalanced, but all he said was, "I'll give you a sleeping pill to help you relax."

The doctor stopped for a moment and looked closely at one of the stone statues.

We paused for a last look at the figures, but as we turned to leave, the doctor stopped for a moment and looked closely at one of the stone statues.

"That's strange," he said. "This one's hand is broken."

I looked and saw what he meant. A finger was missing from the left hand of one of the statues. How had that happened?

"Perhaps some of the village children were playing here," I said, doubtfully, but I didn't really believe it. Children didn't play in the church, and I was sure the stories they heard about the knights frightened them too much to go near the marble figures.

The doctor and I walked together without talking. My friend was thoughtful, but nothing more was said about the missing marble finger.

As we walked up the garden path to my home, we saw a light from the front door, it was open. On entering the house, we saw that the sitting-room door was open, too.

"How strange," I thought. "Did Laura go out?"

The doctor followed me into the room. Huge candles were in glasses and jars all over the room – far more than there were when I went out for my smoke. I wasn't surprised – light was Laura's cure for nervousness.

Then, I saw Laura in the armchair. She had moved it from the fire to the window. Her book was on the floor and her back was to me.

Then, I saw Laura in the armchair.

She had half fallen out of the chair.

"Oh my love, did you wake up and see I was gone?" I wondered. "Did you wait for me and watch through the window?"

Then, I saw the look of fear and horror on her face. Her eyes were wide open in panic.

The doctor moved towards her, but I pushed him aside and ran forward. I caught my darling in my arms and said, "You're safe now, my love. I'm here. You're safe now."

I held her and spoke to her. I called her all the loving names I always used, but I think I knew all the time that she was dead. Her hands were closed and in one of them she held something **tightly**. When I was quite certain she was dead, and that nothing in the world mattered any more, I let the doctor open her hand to see what she was holding.

It was a grey marble finger.

CHAPTERS 3-4 ACTIVITIES

1 Replace the bolded words in the sentences with the words below.

no doubt unlikely mattered missing huge made an effort

1. A **very large** house had once stood on the land.

   ....

2. I had **a feeling of certainty** something was wrong.

   ....

3. She **tried hard** to smile and look happy.

   ....

4. He saw that the marble figures were **not there**.

   ....

5. It was **not very probable** that children played in the church.

   ....

6. After his wife died, nothing **was important** to him.

   ....

2 Complete the sentences in your own words to show you understand the meaning of the words in bold.

1. The doctor said his patient was **overworked** and ....
2. It took several men to **lift** ....
3. I took the **empty** bottle ....
4. There were a lot of **candles** in the room ....
5. His heart began to **beat** fast when ....
6. The church doors were **wide open** ....

Did you know?

In some cultures, people wear lucky amulets as protection against evil spirits. In the past, some Christians marked crosses on the doorways of their houses to keep evil spirits out.

3 Match A to B to form sentences about the story.

A

1. Laura suggested singing duets
2. The narrator left the house
3. The narrator couldn't believe
4. The doctor took his friend to the church
5. Laura felt less nervous

B

.... a. when there was light in a room.
.... b. to prove he was mistaken.
.... c. when the church bell struck 11.00.
.... d. the marble figures were not there.
.... e. to make them feel better.

4 A flashback is a reference to an earlier event that interrupts the chronological order of the story. It gives us important information about the past and about a character. What tragic flashback did Laura describe? How did it affect her mood or behaviour?

....

....

....

5 Answer the questions. Write the answers in your notebook.

1. Why did the narrator go alone to the church?
2. What made the narrator think the legend might be true after all?
3. What was strange about one of the marble statues?
4. Why did the doctor take the narrator home?

The Body Snatcher

by Robert Lewis Stevenson

PRE-READING ACTIVITIES

1 Complete the sentences with the words below.

corpses murdered untied tools disbelief whisper

1. They .... the sack to see what was inside.
2. We had to .... , so no one would hear us.
3. He looked at the dead girl's familiar face in ....
4. Medical students often use .... to learn anatomy.
5. An evil man .... the young woman.
6. Several .... were needed for digging the grave.

2 Surgeons have got very responsible jobs. People trust them with their lives. What kind of person do you think makes a good surgeon?

....

....

....

3 To study anatomy, medical students must dissect bodies. Where do you think medical universities get the bodies from?

....

....

....

The Anatomy Lesson of Dr. Nicolaes Tulp by Rembrandt

CHAPTER 1

A Curious Meeting

Every night, the four of us sat in our private corner in *The George*, in Debenham – the teacher, the landlord, Fettes and myself. Sometimes, we were joined by others, but whatever the weather, the four of us were always there, each sitting in his comfortable armchair.

Unlike the rest of us, Fettes had not grown up in Debenham, but he had been around for years and we accepted him as a local. In fact, we knew very little about him. He was clearly educated and since he had never worked, he was apparently quite rich. Yet, he always wore a very old coat, and looked as if he didn't care about his appearance. We called him 'the doctor' because he had some medical knowledge.

While the rest of us had a couple of drinks, and discussed local politics or the state of the world, Fettes rarely contributed to the conversation. He drank his nightly five glasses of rum, and spent most of the time in a state of silent, alcoholic melancholy.

One dark winter evening, it had already struck nine when the landlord joined us. "Thank Heaven for that," he said, **sighing** deeply. "The doctor is with him now."

Every night, the four of us sat in our private corner in The George.

He was referring to a **guest** who was staying at *The George*. The man had been taken ill while travelling home to London. The landlord had telegraphed the man's London doctor, who came at once.

"What's the doctor's name?" I asked, more out of politeness than out of any real interest.

"MacFarlane, Dr Wolfe MacFarlane," replied the landlord.

To our amazement, Fettes sat straight up in his chair. He looked shocked. "It can't be him," he said. "It can't be. But can there be two doctors with that name?"

He turned to the landlord and asked, "How old is this man?"

"He's got white hair, but looks younger than you," was the reply.

"No. He's older than me. Perhaps he looks younger because he isn't **troubled** by his conscience," said Fettes. "I have a conscience now, but I'm not the good Christian you think I am. I had a good brain once, but I didn't use it. I **sinned**. Oh yes, I sinned."

Then, he turned to the landlord again and said, "I must see this man and know if it's him."

At that moment, a door closed loudly on the floor above us, and the landlord said, "That's the doctor. Hurry – you can see him before he leaves."

We were all curious to know the meaning of Fettes' strange words. We followed him to the stairs, to observe the meeting between the two men. Whatever we expected, it certainly wasn't what we saw. Dr MacFarlane was a confident-looking gentleman, fashionably dressed, with a gold watch chain and round, gold **spectacles**. He walked quickly down the stairs but stopped very suddenly when he saw Fettes. A look of horror crossed his face.

"MacFarlane!" said Fettes, loudly. "Toddy MacFarlane!"

MacFarlane's voice was just a whisper when he said, "Fettes! Is it really you?"

"Indeed it is," said Fettes. "Did you think I was dead, too? No, I'm afraid you can't **get rid of** me so easily."

By now, MacFarlane had regained control of himself, and with a look of pity he said to Fettes, "I see life has been unkind to you. Let me do something for you, for old times' sake."

The doctor put his hand in his pocket and brought out some money. Fettes was furious. "*Money*? Money from *you*?" he shouted. "The money I had from you is lying where I threw it in the rain."

"As you wish," replied MacFarlane, trying to sound dignified, but there was an ugly look on his face as he continued, "I'll leave you my address in case you change your mind."

"*Never*!" shouted Fettes, fiercely. "I'll never contact you! I don't wish to know where you live. I just pray I never see you again."

"I'll never contact you!" shouted Fettes, fiercely. "I just pray I never see you again."

Fettes was standing between the stairs and the front door of *The George*. As the doctor moved towards the door, Fettes pulled his arm and whispered, "Have you seen it again?"

MacFarlane gave a loud cry, pushed Fettes aside and hurried out of the door.

Fettes turned to us and said quietly, "He's a very dangerous man. I mustn't fight him. Those that have argued with him repented too late."

After saying these words, he turned and left. We returned to our corner and sat late into the night by the comfortable fire. Over and over again, we talked of the scene we had witnessed and speculated on the meaning of it. I believe each of us, in our hearts, resolved to discover the secret Fettes shared with the mysterious doctor.

"I'll discover the truth," I promised myself, and that is what I did. But the truth did not bring me any joy. Read on and I will share with you the awful and unnatural events that I discovered.

CHAPTER 2

A Difficult Test

In his youth, Fettes studied at the Edinburgh School of Medicine. Although it is hard to believe it now, he was a good-looking young man. He was intelligent, polite to his superiors and had an excellent memory. He was soon noticed by his teachers, among them Mr K, the popular teacher of anatomy. The students never knew what his full name was – everybody called him Mr K.

Mr K needed a regular supply of bodies for his anatomy students. Fettes admired him greatly and felt **flattered** when Mr K made him his sub-assistant, responsible for the order and cleanliness of the dissecting rooms. It was Fettes' job to receive the bodies, and, together with the **chief** assistant, Dr MacFarlane, distribute body parts for the students to dissect.

It was Fettes' job to receive the bodies.

Mr K never asked his assistants about the supply of bodies. He used to say, "They supply them, we pay for them and that's it." He said it jokingly, but the implication was serious, and very clear – don't ask any more questions.

Supplying corpses was a delicate business in those days, and corpses for dissection were always delivered at night. For that reason, Fettes slept in a room in the same building as the dissecting rooms. He sometimes had to force himself from sleep to accept delivery and pay the **rough-looking** fellows who brought the corpses.

On several occasions, Fettes thought to himself, "This body looks very fresh. It's certainly not long dead," but he said nothing.

If anyone had suggested to Mr K that the subjects were provided by murder, he would have been horrified. If Fettes saw any evidence of crime, he kept quiet. He was an insensitive fellow, and had no interest in the fate of others. His only interests were in satisfying his teacher, enjoying life and succeeding in his studies.

On one occasion, however, Fettes' silence was put to the test. One night, the men brought a body later than usual, and were in a great hurry to leave. Fettes was hardly awake when he lit the men's way to the dissecting room to deliver their large package.

When they put the body on the table, Fettes looked at the face and cried out in shock, "Oh my God! That's Jane Galbraith – I know her! She was alive and well yesterday." He looked suspiciously at the men as he continued, "It's impossible that you got this body honestly."

"You're mistaken," said one of the men. The hostile tone of his voice was clear as he held out his hand to receive his pay.

Fettes' heart beat loudly. He said nothing more, counted out the money and watched his awful visitors depart. He looked again at the corpse, and saw, with horror, marks of violence on her body.

"What should I do?" he asked himself in despair. "What should I do? I don't want to make trouble for Mr K, but I can't keep silent."

Fettes decided to ask MacFarlane for advice. He had travelled a great deal and had seen a lot of things, but he was also unscrupulous. He owned a **gig**, and when more bodies were needed than the men supplied, he drove, in the middle of the night, to lonely cemeteries to steal recently buried bodies.

Fettes showed MacFarlane Miss Galbraith's body.

"It *does* look a bit suspicious," said MacFarlane.

"What should I do?" Fettes wanted to know.

"*Do*?" he repeated. "Why should you *do* anything at all? The less you say or do, the better." He paused for a moment and continued. "Anyway," he said, "*most* of our corpses have been murdered."

"What?" cried Fettes.

"Don't tell me you never suspected it," cried MacFarlane, in disbelief.

"Suspecting is one thing ..." said Fettes.

"Well," said MacFarlane, "I know what I would do. Mr K chose us as his assistants because he believed he could depend on us. I'd do exactly what he expects of us – which is nothing at all."

MacFarlane knew that Fettes wanted Mr K's approval more than anything. He watched Fettes battle very briefly with himself.

"I should do something," thought Fettes. "But on the other hand, it would be wrong of me to make trouble for Mr K."

It didn't take him long to reach a decision. "It's probably best to do nothing," he agreed.

Fettes looked at the face and cried out in shock, "Oh my God! That's Jane Galbraith – I know her!"

With that, he put the problem out of his mind. He and MacFarlane dissected Jane's body, gave the parts to the students the next day and didn't discuss the matter any more.

1 Circle the best continuation for each sentence. Pay attention to the words in bold.

1. The answer brought me great **joy**.
   a. Now I could stop worrying.
   b. I was very upset to hear it.
2. The professor of anatomy was **in despair**.
   a. He had no corpses for students to dissect.
   b. The students were working very well.
3. I never **suspected** the man.
   a. He was always so unpleasant.
   b. I always thought he was honest.
4. The farmer's wife was **buried** the next day.
   a. All the family were very sad.
   b. The doctor said she would recover.
5. The student had to **force himself** to stay awake.
   a. He was exhausted.
   b. He had slept well.

2 Circle the best answer to complete the sentence.

1. I'm sorry you won't accept my help. If you ...., please tell me.
   a. care b. change your mind c. make trouble
2. The famous doctor always looked well dressed and ....
   a. awful b. insensitive c. confident
3. She was very clever and had a lot of general ....
   a. knowledge b. supply c. pity
4. When you finish work, please .... us for a drink.
   a. share b. join c. provide
5. A person who .... a crime should go to the police.
   a. argues b. succeeds c. witnesses

Did you know?

The famous Edinburgh Medical School in Scotland was established nearly 300 years ago as part of Edinburgh University. Graduates of the school have set up some of the most famous medical schools around the world.

3 Who said it? Match the people in A to the correct quote in B.

A

1. The landlord
2. Fettes
3. Mr K
4. MacFarlane
5. The narrator

B

.... a. "Oh my God! That's Jane Galbraith – I know her!"

.... b. "I'll discover the truth."

.... c. "Why should you *do* anything at all? The less you say or do, the better."

.... d. "That's the doctor. Hurry – you can see him before he leaves."

.... e. "They supply them, we pay for them and that's it."

4 We learn about a character in the story by the things they say or do. What do we learn about Fettes based on his decision not to report his suspicions about Jane Galbraith?

....

....

....

5 Answer the questions. Write the answers in your notebook.

1. How did the narrator describe Fettes?
2. How did Fettes describe himself to his drinking friends at *The George*?
3. What mystery was the narrator at *The George* determined to solve?
4. How did Fettes' attitude to the bodies change as a result of MacFarlane's influence?

CHAPTER 3

A Lion or a Lamb?

One day, Fettes finished cleaning the dissecting rooms early and decided to go to a popular tavern for a drink. He was surprised to see MacFarlane there with a tall man with dark hair and dark skin, whom he introduced as Gray. Gray invited Fettes to join them and spoke to him in a friendly manner. But his attitude to MacFarlane was quite different. He treated him like a servant and spoke to him offensively.

"This beer is terrible. Get me something different," he ordered MacFarlane. As soon as MacFarlane sat down again, he said rudely, "Get a drink for our friend here at once," and a few minutes later, "jump up and close that door."

"Why does MacFarlane agree to such treatment?" Fettes wondered. "Why doesn't he react? I don't understand."

Gray ordered a magnificent dinner for the three men, but when he got up after the meal, he looked down at MacFarlane, smiled maliciously and said, "Pay the bill, Toddy."

MacFarlane was clearly furious, but he said nothing. Fettes looked at the expression on MacFarlane's face. "If looks could kill ..." he thought to himself.

Gray looked down at MacFarlane, smiled maliciously and said, "Pay the bill, Toddy."

That night, Fettes was woken by a knock on the door around four o'clock in the morning. He went down to open the door, expecting to see the usual criminals with their horrible sack. The sack looked similar, but it was *MacFarlane* who was carrying it.

"Have you been to the **graveyard** alone?" asked Fettes, greatly surprised. "Why didn't you ask me to go with you?"

"Get on with it," said MacFarlane, abruptly. They carried the heavy sack upstairs to a table and MacFarlane untied the string. Then, he said to Fettes, "I think you should look at the face."

Fettes suddenly trembled with fear. Strange doubts entered his mind as he looked first at MacFarlane, and then very slowly at the face of the corpse. It was Gray – the man he had met with MacFarlane in the tavern. Overcome with shock, Fettes was unable to speak.

"You must pay me for the body," said MacFarlane, calmly.

"Pay you, pay you for *that*!" exclaimed Fettes.

"It's important to keep the records correct," was the answer.

Almost in a dream, Fettes paid him the money and wrote the details in his book. He didn't notice the small smile of relief on MacFarlane's face once the transaction was completed.

"Here," MacFarlane said, giving the money to Fettes. "A bit of unexpected money should make you happy."

"Happy?" said Fettes, furiously. "I've risked my life to **oblige** you."

"To *oblige* me?" cried MacFarlane. "Think what would happen to you if I got into trouble. This little matter is the continuation of Jane Galbraith. You did nothing then, and there's nothing you can do now. You can't stop once you've begun."

A terrible sense of blackness filled Fettes' soul. He sat down and put his head in his hands.

"What have I done?' he whispered, in horror. "What can I do?"

"Be a man and keep your mouth shut," said MacFarlane. "Take the money and enjoy it. In this world, you're either a lion or a lamb. If you're a lamb, you'll end up like this fellow here. You're clever, and you've got courage, Fettes. I like you and Mr K likes you. You were born to be a lion, like me."

He put his hand on Fettes' shoulder as he was leaving and said, "In a few days, all this will be forgotten."

Fettes was left alone with his conscience. It briefly entered his mind that he could go to the police. But the memory of his own part in Jane Galbraith's dissection, and the transaction he had just completed, made him realise that was impossible. He was trapped.

"I've been weak and foolish," he said to himself. "Now I'm a paid accomplice, and there's nothing I can do about it."

"What have I done?" Fettes whispered, in horror. "What can I do?"

For several days, Fettes lived in fear of discovery but as each day passed, he felt a little better. The body was dissected and the parts distributed to the enthusiastic students. Nothing remained to identify the corpse. "It's going to be alright. We're safe," Fettes said to himself, with a sigh of relief.

He began to re-arrange his thoughts until he didn't feel guilty any more. He remembered with pleasure what MacFarlane had said about him. "He thinks I'm clever and brave," thought Fettes. "He likes me and Mr K likes me, too." The thought gave him a warm feeling.

When Fettes met MacFarlane at work, he was pleasant, but he never mentioned their shared secret. He **nodded**, but said nothing when Fettes whispered in his ear, "I've decided to join the lions."

CHAPTER 4

The Only Occupant

A few days later, Mr K was short of bodies again, and news came of the funeral of a farmer's wife in a remote graveyard near Glencorse, south of Edinburgh. It was too good an opportunity to miss.

It was a wet, gloomy day when MacFarlane and Fettes left in the gig, with a bottle of whisky to keep them warm. They planned to first spend the evening in the town of Penicuik, and on the way there they stopped first at the Glencorse cemetery, and hid their tools under some bushes.

Then, they visited Penicuik tavern. Their horses were fed, and MacFarlane and Fettes enjoyed the best meal and wine the place could offer. With every glass of wine, their feeling of satisfaction and companionship grew.

With great warmth, MacFarlane gave some gold to his companion. Fettes put the gold in his pocket, and said happily, "You've made a man of me, MacFarlane."

"That's true," said his companion. "It took a man to help me the way you did with Gray. Instead of being sick or making a fuss, you stayed calm."

"Well, why not?" **boasted** Fettes. "There was nothing to win by causing trouble – and I knew I could count on your gratitude."

MacFarlane felt a touch of alarm. "Have I taught the young fellow a bit too successfully?" he wondered and he became more anxious as Fettes continued, "Who cares about the devil? He may frighten boys, but not men of the world, like you and me."

Finally, it was time to leave. MacFarlane announced that they were going to a place called Peebles, and they drove until they were clear of the last houses. Then, they extinguished the lamps, turned back and took the side roads to Glencorse and the graveyard beyond.

They found the fresh grave of the farmer's wife and turned the gig, so the lamp from the gig illuminated the area. Both men were experienced with the **spade**, and after about 20 minutes of digging, their hit the coffin lid.

They found the fresh grave of the farmer's wife.

They lifted the coffin out and opened it. Then, they put the woman's body into a sack and tied it tightly with string. Fettes sat in the gig and held the sack vertically while MacFarlane climbed into the gig on the other side of the body. He sat down and took the **reins**.

It had rained continually all evening, and by now the corpse and the two men were **soaking wet**. As the gig rolled along the **muddy** road, the wet sack fell from side to side, sometimes resting its head on a shoulder. The men could not avoid it, and the horrible contact began to affect their nerves. To make matters worse, the light from their lamp was weakening.

As they passed the farms along the route, the farm dogs began to howl at them in a frightening way.

"Why do they all howl at us like that?" Fettes wondered. "It's like they feel something evil is happening."

Strange thoughts began to cross Fettes' mind. The rain had **moulded** the sack to the head and body of the corpse. It seemed to Fettes that the corpse had changed shape – it was much bigger than before! An idea entered his mind that something unnatural and sinister had occurred inside the sack, and the dogs were howling out of fear of the unholy creature next to them.

It seemed to Fettes that the corpse had changed shape – it was much bigger than before!

After a while, the light from their lamp went out and they stopped the gig. With great difficulty, in the pouring rain, they managed to re-light it. They could see the sack more clearly now. Horror attacked both men.

"This is not a woman's body," MacFarlane whispered.

"It was a woman when we put her in," Fettes replied, fearfully.

"Hold the lamp! I must see the face!" MacFarlane cried, hysterically.

As Fettes took the lamp, MacFarlane untied the sack and pulled it down. The light fell on a familiar dark-skinned face.

Wild screams rang through the night as each man jumped from his side of the gig onto the road. The lamp fell to the ground and broke. The horse, terrified by the unusual sounds, galloped on towards Edinburgh, taking with it the only occupant of the gig – the body of the dead and long-dissected Gray.

CHAPTERS 3-4 ACTIVITIES

1 Complete the puzzle using the sentences as clues.

Across ▶

3. I didn't understand the man's unkind .... of Dr MacFarlane.
6. Fettes and MacFarlane ate and their horses were ....

Down ▼

1. Fettes was worried. If people thought he was .... of a crime, he would go to prison.
2. Fettes felt ashamed that he was not .... enough to report the murder to the police.
4. Fettes waited for the doctor beside the front door, so the doctor couldn't .... seeing him.
5. The body snatchers were careful not to behave in a suspicious ....

2 Find eight words in the puzzle. Then use the them to complete the sentences below.

howledtrappedbillintroducedstringunexpecteddigmanaged

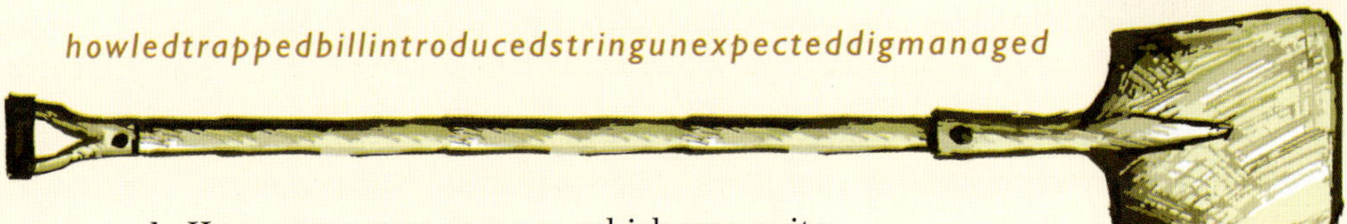

1. He gave me some money, which was quite ....
2. It was difficult to hold the sack, but we ....
3. We put the books in a sack and tied it with ....
4. It was very scary when the dogs ....
5. We had to .... a deep hole in the ground.
6. The professor .... his assistants to each other.
7. After the delicious meal, my friend paid the ....
8. I was .... in a terrible situation and could do nothing.

3 Match each sentence beginning in A to the correct ending in B.

A

1. At a popular tavern, Fettes met
2. MacFarlane was angry when he got
3. Fettes was horrified to see
4. MacFarlane was anxious to complete
5. After a while, Fettes overcame
6. The howling dogs frightened
7. Late at night, the two men entered
8. The sack didn't contain

B

.... a. his bad feelings.
.... b. the men in the gig.
.... c. the country cemetery.
.... d. a woman's body, any more.
.... e. a face he recognised.
.... f. the sale of the corpse.
.... g. MacFarlane and Gray.
.... h. an unfair order.

4 A motive is the reason for a person's actions. What was the motive for each of these actions? Write the answers in your notebook.

1. MacFarlane told Fettes to pay him for the body and record the transaction.
2. The two men stopped at the cemetery before they drove to Penicuik.
3. In the Penicuik tavern, MacFarlane announced they were going to Peebles.
4. On the way home, the men stopped the gig in the pouring rain.
5. The men decided to open the sack with the body in it.

Did you know?

In 1828, William Burke and William Hare were accused of murdering 16 people in Edinburgh and selling their bodies to Dr Robert Knox for students to dissect in his anatomy lectures. Burke was hanged, but Hare was released after he gave evidence against Burke.

GLOSSARY

The Signal-Man

English	Castellano	Català
betray	traicionar	trair
compelled	obligado	obligat
cutting	desmonte	desmunt, rebaix
distressed	afligido, angustiado	afligit, angoixat
duty	deber	deure
earn a living	ganarme la vida	guanyar-me la vida
faded	se desvaneció / perdió	es va esvair / perdre
fateful	fatídicas	fatídiques
gloomy	sombrío, lúgubre	ombrívol, llòbrec
inn	posada	fonda, hostal
Look out!	¡Cuidado!	Atenció!
mood	estado de ánimo	estat d'ànim
mourning	duelo	dol
nightmare	pesadilla	malson
overcome	superado, dominado	aclaparat, dominat
relieved	aliviado	alleugerit
rough	irregular, lleno de baches	irregular, ple de sots
second sight	clarividencia	clarividència
signal box	garita de señales	garita (del guardaagulles)
steep	empinado	costerut
unbalanced	trastornada	desequilibrada
wasted	perdí	vaig perdre
waved	agitaba	feia senyals amb
willingly	de buen grado	de bon grat, de gust

GLOSSARY

English	Euskara	Galego
betray	traizionatu	traizoar
compelled	mesedibat egin	obrigado
cutting	ebakitako mendi-zati	desmonte
distressed	atsekabetuta, nahigabetuta	aflixido, agoniado
duty	betebehar	deber
earn a living	bizitza atera	gañar a vida
faded	deuseztatu / desagertu zen	se esvaeceu / perdeu
fateful	zoritxarreko	fatídicas
gloomy	laiotz, ilun	sombrío, avesedo, lúgubre
inn	ostatu	pousada
Look out!	Kontuz!	Coidado!
mood	aldarte	estado de ánimo
mourning	dolu	dó
nightmare	amesgaizto	pesadelo
overcome	gaindituta	superado, animado
relieved	lasaituta	aliviado, acalmado
rough	zuloz betetako	irregular, cheo de fochancas
second sight	iragarmen	clarividencia
signal box	seinaleen garita	garita de sinais
steep	maldatsu	costento, empinado
unbalanced	nahasita	trastornada, anubrada
wasted	galdu nuen	perdín
waved	astintzen zuen	axitaba
willingly	gogo onez	de bo grado

GLOSSARY

The Marble Finger

English	Castellano	Català
aisle	nave (lateral)	nau lateral
All Saints' Eve	la víspera del Día de Todos los Santos	la vigília de Tot Sants
carved	esculpidas	esculpides
choked	me ahogaba / asfixiaba	m'ofegava
churchyard	cementerio	cementiri
coffin	de ataúd	de taüt
estate agents	agentes inmobiliarios	agents de la propietat immobiliària
evil deeds	malas acciones	males accions
grasped	agarrados	agafats
heirs	herederos	hereus
hesitated	dudó	va dubtar
housekeeping	tareas de la casa	tasques de la llar
insane	loco	boig
marble	(de) mármol	(de) marbre
playing a trick	gastando una broma	fent una broma
poacher	cazador furtivo	caçador furtiu
relief	alivio	alleujament
spire	aguja, chapitel	agulla, fletxa
struck	alcanzó; dio	va caure; va tocar
tightly	con fuerza	amb força

GLOSSARY

English	Euskara	Galego
aisle	(alboko) nabe	nave (lateral)
All Saints' Eve	Santu Guztien Egunaren bezperan	a véspera do Día de Todos os Santos
carved	zizelkatuta	esculpidas
choked	ito egin nintzen	me afogaba / asfixiaba
churchyard	hilerri	cemiterio
coffin	hilkutxa	de ataúde
estate agents	higiezinen agente(ak)	axentes inmobiliarios
evil deeds	ekintza maltzur(rak)	malas accións
grasped	eutsi (ta)	agarrados
heirs	oinordeko(ak)	herdeiros
hesitated	zalantza egin zuen	dubidou
housekeeping	etxeko lanak	tarefas da casa
insane	erotuta	tolo, louco
marble	marmol	(de) mármore
playing a trick	ziria sartzen	gastando unha brincadeira
poacher	isileko ehiztari	cazador furtivo
relief	lasaitasun	alivio
spire	orratz	agulla, chapitel
struck	jo zuenean; jo zituen	acadou, alcanzou; deu
tightly	indarrez	con forza

GLOSSARY

The Body Snatcher

English	Castellano	Català
boasted	alardeó	va presumir
chief	del jefe	del cap
flattered	halagado	afalagat
get rid of	deshacerte de	desfer-te / lliurar-te de
gig	calesa	calessa
graveyard	cementerio	cementiri
guest	huésped	hoste
moulded	moldeado, dado forma a	donat forma a
muddy	llena de barro	enfangada
nodded	asintió con la cabeza	va dir que sí amb el cap
oblige	hacer un favor	fer un favor
reins	riendas	regnes
rough-looking	de aspecto tosco / rudo	d'aspecte matusser
sighing	suspirando	sospirant
sinned	he pecado	he pecat
soaking wet	empapados	xops
spade	pala	pala
spectacles	gafas	ulleres
troubled	inquieto	inquiet

GLOSSARY

English	Euskara	Galego
boasted	harrokeriaz esan zuen	alardeou
chief	buru(aren), nagusi(aren)	do xefe
flattered	lausengatuta	afagado
get rid of	begien bistatik kendu	desfacerte de
gig	kalesa	carruaxe
graveyard	hilerri	cemiterio
guest	apopilo	hóspede
moulded	moldekatu, forma eman	moldeado, dado forma a
muddy	lokatzez beteta	chea de lama
nodded	buruarekin baietsi zuen	asentiu coa cabeza
oblige	mesede bat egin	facer un favor
reins	brida(k)	rendas
rough-looking	itxura zakar	de aspecto rudo / basto
sighing	hasperen eginaz	suspirando
sinned	bekatu egin nuen	pequei
soaking wet	blai	enchoupados
spade	pala	pa
spectacles	betaurreko(ak)	lentes
troubled	urdurituta, atsekabetuta	inquedo

GHOSTS IN DIFFERENT CULTURES

What do you imagine when you think of a ghost? Some people imagine ghosts which are invisible, but their presence can be 'felt'. Others imagine something like a delicate cloud without a definite shape, and still more people imagine a figure that looks very much like the person when they were alive.

Different cultures have got different beliefs, not only about the form ghosts take, but also about their intentions.

In Chinese culture, for example, people believe that the ghosts of ancestors return to Earth. If they have been disrespected in life, they will want to cause **harm** to the living. The Chinese perform rituals to prevent this from happening. They also perform rituals to keep benevolent ghosts happy, so they will continue to be friendly to their families. Similar beliefs and rituals exist in Japan and in several other Asian and African countries.

In other cultures, ghosts are often believed to be spirits of people who died tragically. Some people believe the spirits can't 'rest', so they return to **haunt** the place where they died. One common ghostly figure in many western cultures is the 'white lady'. Typically, she is a lady who lost her husband, or whose husband or lover betrayed her. Her appearance is understood to be a warning that someone is going to die. One of the most famous examples is the Irish banshee, whose appearance predicts the death of a member of an Irish family.

Sceptics and scientists try to find rational explanations for ghosts. They are not always successful, so we are still left with the unanswered question: Do ghosts really exist?

harm	daño	mal	kalte, min	dano
haunt	aparecerse en, rondar	aparèixer a, rondar per	(n) agertu / inguruan ibili	aparecerse en, roldar

1 **Find evidence in the text that supports the following statements about ghosts and complete the chart.**

Statement	Evidence
1 Different people have got different ideas about the form ghosts have.	
2 Some Chinese believe people who were treated badly are dangerous after they die.	
3 China is not the only place where people hold ceremonies to influence ghosts.	
4 A 'white lady' is considered a bad sign.	
5 There are people who try to prove that ghosts don't exist.	

2 **Complete the sentences according to the text.**

1. People may be aware of a ghost nearby even if ....
2. The Chinese perform rituals to influence both ....
3. A restless ghost is the spirit of a person who ....
4. The Irish banshee is one example of ....
5. Without definite proof, we don't know ....

HALLOWEEN

Western Christian societies usually celebrate Halloween (All Hallows' Eve) on 31st October, the evening before All Saints' Day, which is on 1st November. However, a great many Halloween celebrations today have very little to do with saints or religion.

The origin of Halloween is uncertain. Many believe it originated from the pagan Celtic festival of Samhain. On that day, Celts gave thanks for the **harvest**, which marked the end of summer and also remembered their dead. They believed that the spirits of the dead returned as ghosts. The Celts lit fires and wore ugly masks and witches' costumes to scare these evil spirits away.

Many Halloween superstitions and customs are connected to spirits or with death. In Ireland and Scotland, children in costumes carry **lanterns** with faces carved from large **turnips** to frighten evil spirits. Another superstition is not to look over your shoulder on Halloween, as it brings bad luck. Another belief is that people born on Halloween can see into the future.

Some old Halloween customs have changed over the years. In the past, poor people used to knock on doors of houses and beg for food. They called the food 'soul cakes' because in return for it, they promised to pray for the souls of dead members of the house. Today, children in costumes knock on doors and are given sweets. They often shout 'trick or treat', pretending they will play a trick on the house owner if they don't give them some sweets.

Halloween has become more and more popular over the years, and today it is a time for parties, celebrations and fun in many countries. In New York, for example, tens of thousands of people in costumes and masks take part in a festive **parade** on Halloween night.

harvest	cosecha	collita	uzta	colleita
lanterns	faroles	fanals	argiontzi(ak), farol(ak)	farois
turnips	nabos	naps	arbi(ak)	nabos
parade	desfile	desfilada	desfile	desfile